I0518683

Copyright 2021, *Ely's Gift.*

All rights reserved.

This is an Early Chapter Book, published by Lombosco Publications, Canada.

Date Published: May 3, 2021

Dedication

This Early Chapter Book is dedicated-

To my Mom who is my number 1 fan;

To Susana Gener,

a friend who believes in my writing ability;

to my three high school friends whom I call "fairies"- Teodora, Isabel and Minerva;

And to my "Little Cherubims".

Table of Contents

Foreword

I first met *Author Lucy Lombos* while taking up graduate studies in Education where I have already been captivated by her kindness, friendliness and charm. Allow me to call her Lutchie. That's how I dearly call her. I also feel comfortable to call her sweet, local nickname.

As we went through the rigors of studying for our courses under the most demanding professors, Lutchie has been a source of much delight and inspiration to me and our classmates. Not only did she enlghten us with her rich insights during class discussions, she always reached out to amuse or comfort us, and share her words of encouragement and wisdom. She was our class mother and «guiding light», as any Luz (her real name) like her should rightfully be.

Fast forward to 2020, Lutchie is now happily settled in Canada and the author of more than a dozen children's books, including her fables, a biography and a novel. It is wonderful to read her books and be imbued once again by the beauty and magic of Lutchie's person in her writings. Every character and plot in her stories tend to captivate the imagination, touch the heart and educate the mind to universal values in life: kindness, humility, respect, love and sacrifice for family or friends, among others.

Lutchie's latest book offering, «Ely's Gift», continues to follow her distinct style and tradition. In a story set in the magical fairy kingdom of Verde Hilltop, a little fairy-in-the making named Ely will lead us to discover the most precious gift that would rightfully befit their beloved Queen Isabella.

As a parent and early childhood educator, I understand our need to provide quality literature to our children and students with the hope that not only would it be enjoyable, but it would also leave something worthwhile to them. «Ely's Gift» would truly be a gift that not only entertains but also helps shape them towards becoming loving and worthy citizens in this world. Read, enjoy and be transformed by Lutchie's latest gift to us!

- Sining Tañedo Bruni, MA, Med
International Preschool Teacher
and Heritage Language Advocate,
Basel, Switzerland

Wings, smiles and tears

can change everything.

Lucy Lombos

Ely's Gift

Illustrated by Nisansala Alwis

Chapter 1- Fallen Angels?

"Is it true that we are called fallen angels?" Ely asked.

"Bah, who told you that?" Auggie replied.

"My best friend!" Ely answered while she was braiding her hair in two.

"Hmmm... maybe, he was just making fun of you," Auggie gave his comment to his darling daughter.

"That's not true, my little one! Fairies are part of this world," Dorie, who flapped her old rosy, greenie wings up and down as if she would fly, shared her opinion to her one and only daughter with dimples on her both cheeks.

In that early afternoon, they heard a loud sound of a trumpet, calling all fairies and other creatures with wings in Verde Hilltop.

The first Monday of the month is the general assembly of the fairies. It is usually done in late afternoon before the sun sets. All of them gather at the top of the breathtaking Verde Hilltop. It is a dwelling place of enchantment. It is a glittering, botanic wonderland where trees and vegetables grow, and flowers bloom a lot; plentiful enough to feel that there is no end of richness and mysterious beauty. Magic, sweet scent, food, drinks, music and merriments are all abouncing. The fairyland creates a high sprightly energy, unlimited growth and prosperity.

Daisy is one of the fairies' favorite flowers.

Chapter 2- The Advice

"Are you ready?" Auggie asked his beautiful wife while his silvery-misted-greenie wings flitted.

"Yes, I am! And you, Little Ely?" Dorie, who had her hair twisted into ringlets, asked her daughter.

"I'm good! Look, I'm wearing my yellow dress; and I already put on my beige sandals which I tied and crisscrossed its laces up to my knees. But I don't have a pair of green wings for little children my age yet," Ely wondered.

"Be patient! You will have them soon. Remember, you get green wings as you do good deeds. You're doing great as a sevenyear-old fairy," Auggie told his daughter, whose eyes always smile and lips are as red as the rosebuds in the garden.

"Just continue to spread joy, kindness and love. You'll be a full-fledged fairy in no time!" Dorie advised Ely.

"Got it! Yes, I promise to keep doing that," Ely nodded and gave her sweet smiles to her fascinating parents.

The winged-family flew to attend and to report to the exalted Queen at the Verde Hilltop's quadrangle.

Chapter 3- The Announcement

The native dwellers chatted while waiting for the Queen.

Shortly after, Queen Isabella came out from the well-arranged floral and leafy arch, while fluttering her green wings with a shade and unique touch of royal blue color around them. In elegant position, she stood on the stage which was decorated with so many clusters of posies, daisies and roses. The adornment was highlighted by the creeping, red, yellow and green vines that matched her good looks and grace.

"I am here to say my usual, quick greetings. I have not seen most of you, and I just want to see how you are all doing," Queen Isabella began to speak. She styled her hair up like a bun that really looked great, fit for a woman of nobility. Sometimes, she just let her hair down and loose.

The people cheered to show their love and respect for the Queen. The dwellers' chattering built up and the sound rose into a high volume.

"We're all doing well! Thank you, your Majesty!" the crowd all together shouted with so much delight.

"Excellent! From my heart, I wish you all well. Stay safe at all times," Queen Isabella said, loud enough to be heard and then, she waved goodbye to everyone.

Her sincere smile was enough to warm the hearts of all. Afterwards, she left the center of the stage, leaving a short yet positive impression.

The people in the quadrangle stayed a bit when the Queen exited because they seemed mesmerized, looking at the charm and fair beauty of their beloved Queen.

When they started to move, Sammy, the handsome and vigorous fairy member of the Queen's court, appeared. Much the same as the hurled arrow, he took the stage. The talk of the town, a robust soldier, the brave protector of the whole Verde Hilltop, and the secret crush of many female fairies... Those were the buzzing descriptions of the dwellers for Sammy.

The fairies and insects stopped on their tracks. They became curious.

"In three days, it will be the Queen's birthday," Sammy announced with his powerful voice.

All whispered with glee, "Oh, yes, Her Majesty the Queen's special day!"

"Isn't it exciting?" Sammy stimulated the crowd.

"Yes, we love it!" everyone answered in unison.

"Now, please listen up! There will be a Verde Grand Challenge. Think of a great gift not only for the Queen but also for the whole Verde Hilltop," Sammy continued.

Everyone was delighted and was enthu-

siastic about participating in the yearly event.

"Yippee, Verde Hilltop will be quite aglow and radiant at night time once again. How I love it!" Billy, the firefly fairy, remarked.

"When is the assembly time?" Dorie asked.

Chapter 4-

The Past, the Future, the Real Love and Pure Joy

"The Assembly time is at 6:00 in the evening... Any more questions?" Sammy asked.

Auggie raised his hand and asked, "Sammy, what will be the prize to the family who can give the best gift?"

Sammy replied, "A magical crystal ball to foretell someone's future or access to one's past, and especially his real love and pure joy for the Queen and for all the dwellers of Verde Hilltop!

"What's our theme for this year?" Auggie asked for the second time.

"Obviously and significantly, it is the combination of the past and the future, and the most important elements are real love and pure joy! Okay? That's our theme! I won't repeat it anymore."

"That's wonderful! I will take note of the theme. Thanks, Sammy," Auggie said.

Then, speedy Sammy disappeared before another question was asked.

The Queen heard everything while she hid in her regal room. The sweet and lovely blooms from the splendid garden of her place embellished the Queenly throne at her room. Raised on a dais, a huge, purple chair could be seen as her magisterial seat with the ancient fairy's golden wings of power attached at its back.

"Hmmm… No one knows that for this year, I would love the child's tears, out of real love, as part of the making of the precious gift to the entire Verde Hilltop and to me as the birthday celebrator. The gift should give everyone pure joy. Let me see the family who can do that," Queen Isabella secretly thought, and she also became excited.

The assembly was in great awe, thinking of the best gift for the Queen. Each of them went home and began to test their magical powers. The Grand Challenge stirred their creativity. It increased their love for the Queen and their habitat.

Chapter 5- Miggy, the Bee

"Isn't it a short, so abrupt notice, dad?" Ely asked her father.

"We still have time," Auggie said with calmness.

"What do you think, mom?"

"Well, Little Ely, we can use and blend our powers to come up with one priceless gift," Dorie suggested.

Ely kept quiet while her parents started thinking of their gift to their Queen.

The next day, while everybody was busy, Ely jumped and leaped around the sunflowers in the garden. She saw one of her friends.

"Hi Miggy! How are you?" Ely asked.

"I'm good! This is the time of the year that I'm swamped with pollinating works," Miggy buzzed and made a delightful bee line to amuse Ely.

"Wow!... You are a hardworking bee!"

"That's my nature!"

"Keep spreading the pollens. You help a lot of fairies."

"I will... thanks!

"You're welcome!.. Well, I have to go now."

"Hey, don't go far!"

"Thank you, fay-insect!"

Ely praised Miggy. The smiling fairy didn't notice that the lower tip of her wings became green.

In sunny and breezy days, Ely used up most of her time by flying and playing. Having enough time, she went to the rose garden, one of her favorite spots. And before long, she hopped into the white, bridal bouquets. She flew back to the gorgeous rose garden. There, she met another close friend.

Chapter 6-

Mindy, the Monarch Butterfly

"Hello there, fairy Mindy!" Ely greeted her friend.

"Oh, hello!" Fairy Mindy, the fay-Monarch Butterfly greeted her, too.

"How are you, dearest fairy?" Ely asked, giving a bunch of smiles towards her fairy friend.

"I'm good... And yourself?" Mindy replied.

"I'm pretty good. I can see that you are very busy."

"Yeah, it's springtime, you know!" Mindy liked the small talk.

"Enjoy, fay-Monarch Butterfly!" Then, Ely reminded her, "Make sure you take care of yourself, please?"

"Oh, you are really a sweet, dimpled fairy!"

"Fairies should always be kind."

"I agree with you, Ely."

"Thank you."

"You're welcome!"

And then, she flew away...

The green color in her wings started to spread out a bit upward. She went on her way home, not noticing the change.

She kept herself busy as well. Aside from flying and playing, she loved smiling, smelling flowers and learning something new. She also loved visiting, helping and greeting her friends and everyone she would meet. That was all for Ely on the first day after the assembly.

Chapter 7- Billy, the Firefly

On the second day after the assembly, Ely woke up. She helped her mom do the household chores. Then, late in the afternoon, she went to the porch of their tiny tree house. To her surprise, she saw her friend perched on a flower of the tree.

"Hello, fallen angel!" Billy teased Ely.

"Hello! What brings you here?" Ely asked her fairy-insect buddy.

"I just like to play at the treetop. Would you like to play with me?" Billy, with fay-dark green and blue wings, invited Ely.

"Yes! I am thrilled to do that as well.

Let's go!" Ely agreed.

Since Ely and Billy were very young, they have been playing around the treetop. On that beautiful day, they did the same thing that made them so happy. They flew, hopped, and skipped... They were so carefree. Soon, they went into different directions and flew everywhere.

The two fairy buddies were so happy that they forgot the time. Also, they didn't notice that they were already inside the bat cave at the outskirt of the fairies' abode.

Then, all of a sudden, they heard the cave's entrance closed. They also sensed the flapping of huge wings inside the cave. They could feel the creatures of the dark were approaching them.

Ely felt nervous and scared while Billy, being a male firefly fairy, got startled but not panic-stricken.

They readied their wings and flapped them from side to side.

Chapter 8- The Wicked Queen

"Who are you?" a big and ugly flying creature of the dark emerged and asked them.

"We're fairies! We're from the Verde Hilltop," the night buddies answered.

"Aah, from the paradise of the fairies!"

"We're sorry to get inside your cave," Ely and Billy apologized.

"I'm Queen Sonora. I'm the powerful Queen of the Bats. Are you spying me on what to give to your own Queen?"

"Oh, no! We just got lost," Billy, who showed bravery, explained.

"Huh, I'm going to make an extraordinary soup to vanish your Queen," the wicked Queen voiced out.

"Oh no, please, Queen Sonora!" begged Ely.

"No one can stop me!" Queen Sonora warned them.

"Please don't do that!" Ely begged for the second time while Billy listened with courage.

Queen Sonora ignored Ely.

"Shhh... Let's get out of here," Billy whispered. Ely nodded in silence.

Both of them readied themselves to back off when they got jittered to see the army of bats coming inside the cave in haste.

"Queen Sonora, we have some more captives!" one of the bats reported in advance.

Chapter 9- The Ingredients

Not too long, the army of bats entered the cave with Miggy and Mindy as their captives.

"Why are you here?" Ely asked.

"We are looking for you. Our powers led us here," Miggy and Mindy reasoned out.

"Oh, we're in big trouble now," Billy said.

"We can help each other," Mindy calmed them.

"Quick! We have to plan our exit," Miggy whispered.

While the three fairy-insects were planning to break free from the cave, Queen Sonora prepared the cauldron of water.

Ely saw Queen Isabella laid all the ingredients on the table. She spotted the roots from the so-called Judas' tree...

... There were deadly mushrooms,

... Three hair or fur-locks of the beast bat,

... Nectar,

... Bitter herbs,

... Squash,

... Pieces of blue flowers, and so many more.

Besides, she identified a bottle of poison.

She couldn't hold her emotions and started to sob. Her tears flowed down her cheeks, and all looked like a river from her eyes. Her chin and hands trembled, too.

Chapter 10- The Tears

"Why are you crying?" Queen Sonora asked Ely.

"I pity our fair Queen Isabella. I love her and I do not want her to be harmed. Please do not make her disappear!" Ely replied. Her eyes were already red and swollen.

"That is not important now."

"She rules, guides and cares for all the dwellers of Verde Hilltop."

"I do not care!"

"I'm telling the truth."

"It does not matter what you say."

"She makes us happy!"

"Silence!"

"She has a good heart... I love her so much and everyone at the Hilltop loves her, too."

"Nonsense!"

Ely cried and cried, producing a loud sound that could be heard even outside the cave.

"Perhaps, your tears in the cauldron could be a wonderful ingredient to what I am making," Queen Sonora thought.

The beastly Queen used her black magic and collected a few droplets of Ely's tears. Without second thoughts, she put the tears in the hot cauldron.

"Ha ha ha! Your tears will give a special taste... Ha ha ha!" Queen Sonora laughed.

When Ely was still sobbing, Billy whispered to her, "Hey, Ely! Look at your wings!"

Chapter 11- The Reason

Ely's wings became partially green. But she didn't look at her wings. She was determined to know the wicked way of Queen Sonora.

"Maybe we can talk about this... Why do you want our Queen to vanish?" asked Ely, even though her throat was a bit tightened.

"Because to many, she is the only important creature!... Always the lovely one, huh! She is loved by the fairies, it makes me sick!" Queen Sonora pointed out in an angry and envious tone.

"But you have an army of bats and they obey you."

"They obey out of fear!"

"I think if you try to be kinder, they will also love you. A kind and beautiful heart is better than a beautiful face."

"Enough! You're wasting my time!"

"Please listen to my words. You are special and gifted, too! Let your goodness shine while you still have time."

"It's too late... I will make things hard for you!"

"Please, I beg you!" Ely cried out. Afterwards, she took a deep breath.

Then, Queen Sonora kept quiet and went farther away from Ely and her tiny friends. One thing was sure, she would like to continue her evil plan.

Chapter 12- The Rescue

"We have to get out of here," Ely suggested, "We can use your magic."

"Aside from my power, the light on my back will guide us. I can flash it! For sure, it will blind them," Billy said.

"I will cover you with my Monarch wings, hindering them from coming near you," Mindy said.

"I can create a super loud noise, making them panic and sick," Miggy buzzed.

"As of now, since my wings are not yet all green, I don't have the super bewitching power yet. I don't have much to offer here, but my love for the Queen. She should not fall into Queen Sonora's wicked plot," Ely remarked.

"Let's all do this!" the three fay-insects altogether snapped.

Because earlier, Ely cried like a blast while talking to Queen Sonora, the host of fairies, led by Sammy, was able to track them. Everyone, including Auggie and Dorie, mightily entered and brightened the cave. In a hurry, they rescued Ely and her fay-insect friends.

Queen Sonora got mad and scolded her army of bats. Her madness seemed like the boiling water at the cauldron. She reached her boiling point as well.

Soon, with all the fairies' forces, their magical powers and with the he p of the clouds of sparkling specks of dust, everyone got home just in time before twelve midnight. Ely and her parents reached their home and felt very exhausted, too.

Columbine is another favorite flower of the fairies.

Chapter 13- Totally Green

"Where did you really go?" Auggie asked Ely.

"Tell us what happened," Dorie urged her daughter.

"I'm sorry, dad and mom! Billy and I played outside till we reached the bats' cave."

"We were not able to make our gift to the Queen," Auggie remarked.

"I know, dad. What shall we do now?"

Dorie worried a lot yet she suggested, "Let's wait for all of them to present their gifts. We will be at the end of the line."

"That's a good idea, mom!" Ely said.

"Hey, your wings are totally green," Dorie noticed.

"Can I be the gift to our Queen?" asked Ely.

"Having green wings is the sign of spreading kindness, and that's real love and pure joy! You did it, Ely; and that's the past, braving the future," Auggie enlightened them.

"But I'm scared of the Queen of the Bats," Ely brought out her fear.

"Forget about her for now," Dorie said.

"Hmmm, I like the idea!" Auggie said.

"I am now a full-fledged fairy!" Ely declared with so much joy.

"And why not? You can be our gift!" her parents said and their eyes sparkled.

Cowslip is another favorite flower of the fairies.

Chapter 14- The Birthday Gifts

The birthday of Queen Isabella came. Each family lined up. They observed three meters apart from each other so as not to touch their wings. They would also like to have their personal spaces and a shining moment to give the gift.

One family presented to their lovely Queen a golden clock with the female child's voice to remind all dwellers five minutes before eight o'clock in the evening. And if the clock strikes the official, curfew time, all must stay home with the family. Nobody should go out anymore for their protection from the invaders of their abode.

Another family gave a bracelet of jaded charms to ward off evil spirits. They made several bracelets for everybody.

The third family gave boxes of soaps to protect everyone from dirt and other germs that they might get while working, planting, cleaning, and eating; and of course, while dancing, singing and playing.

The fourth family gave lots of sealed plates of ambrosia, fairies' favorite food.

The fifth family offered baskets of lemons and other citrus fruits to make everyone healthy.

The sixth family played a sweet piece of music enjoyed by all with the message to spread love and kindness, and protect the Verde Hilltop, seeing their past and their future.

Others brought bows and arrows, tinkling bells, several flying shoes, and an enchanted mirror to look good all the time.

The fay—insects just did a march-parade to cheer the Queen with the promise to help in the garden and to bring peace.

Many dwellers did their best to make the birthday celebration a wonderful one and beneficial to all.

But wait, the Queen waited for another family who was familiar to her.

Chapter 15- The Poem

"Mom and Dad, please give me a favor. Allow me to recite a poem. I'll do this because I don't like you to be embarrassed. My poem is also our gift," Ely said.

"Do it at once. We are here as one family," Auggie said.

"We love you, Ely!" Dorie pronounced with assuring care and support.

"Look, your wings are now brightly green!" Auggie noticed.

"Wow, that's fantastic!" Ely's mom commented.

"You did an amazing deed of real love!" Auggie remarked.

"Thank you! But I have to change a bit some lines in my poem which I composed at the crack of dawn. So, please give me time to think," Ely said.

"You can do it!" Auggie encouraged his daughter.

"You are smart in writing and reciting poems," Dorie reassured her daughter.

Later on, Ely and her family dashed to the hall.

"It's now your turn," Queen Isabella addressed it to Auggie, Dorie and Ely.

Without much ado, Ely recited her poem.

"Today,

Your majesty's birthday marks my wings fully green,

Now, I have these wings b'cause my heart says, I love you;

Full-fledged fay with green wings, I look pure and sheen,

Playing with wee friends; doing kindness, that's my view.

Yesterday,

In a devil's cave, black creatures, a secret they hid,

Exposed; mind stretched, heart ached, trouble I knew,

The evil soup shouldn't be tasted; I cried as a young kid,

A secret brought tears that equaled love that was true.

Tomorrow,

The learning experience will remind the greening glow,

Sure to save you, adored Queen, I'll never let you vanish,

In uncertainties like this, listen, end with joy, not sorrow,

Real love, I'll give to you, even to one who's outlandish."

After the poem recitation, Ely bowed and made a curtsy to Queen Isabella.

All the dwellers cheered for her. They thought and just felt that something great would happen any minute.

"With tears?... That was what I thought," Queen Isabella remembered.

Chapter 16-
Queen Sonora's Gift

Ely's mother was deeply touched. Hearing the poem, she shed tears.

"Now, we realize that you are the amazing gift to our Queen and to all of us," Auggie and Dorie told Ely.

Right after that, Dorie stole a moment and said, "I'm sorry to interrupt, you, our Majesty. Little Ely got lost in the woods yesterday and she reached the bats' cave. It took us long to find her. For that reason, we were not able to come up with a gift but her truthful poem just for you."

"And look!... She is indeed our precious gift to you. She has transformed into a full-fledged fairy. Her wings are now completely green," Auggie announced.

"I'm sorry; I didn't know this happened to you," Queen Isabella was astounded and she said, "But I'm so glad to see that her wings are now all green. It implies something significant."

Soon after the conversation, at the hush of the moment, Queen Sonora and her army of bats flew at a great speed.

"Am I late? Ha ha ha… Here, I brought the most satisfying gift, the best soup ever. Everyone will have a grand feast with my special soup," Queen Sonora presented her gift in pretension.

"Soup? That must be really special!" the dwellers in unison said.

"This will make you healthy and happy!" the beast Queen bat tempted Queen Isabella and everyone.

At that point, Queen Isabella received the gift. She knew what she was doing.

And everyone heard the sound of repeated NO's uttered by Ely, "No... no, please!" Her tears welled up in her eyes.

Chapter 17-
Queen Isabella's Faith

"No! Don't sip it," Ely warned Queen Isabella, and her tears escaped once again, streaming down on her feverish face.

"We were captivated by the bats," Billy, Miggy and Mindy cried aloud.

"Taste it, Queen Isabella! Don't listen to them!" Queen Sonora shouted out. Then, she scowled at Ely and her friends.

Their loving Queen accepted the bowl of soup.

Lowering her head, Queen Isabella remarked, "I will not become invisible." So, she tasted it with much faith. She had another spoonful of it.

Witnessed by all, Queen Isabella was fine and did not vanish.

"Ha, what happened? You should have disappeared right this very moment," Queen Sonora said in disturbed voice.

"Why, what did you put here?" Queen Isabella asked in a way of having steady power and strength.

"It's exceptional; no one could ever think of it!" Queen Sonora replied.

"I am intrigued! So, what were the ingredients in your special soup?" Queen Isabella asked.

"Your Majesty, I saw them all!" Ely announced and showed her courage, "Queen Sonora put toxic ingredients, such as a bottle of poison and deadly mushrooms."

Queen Sonora gave a beastly glance to Ely.

"You better keep your mouth shut, little fairy!" Queen Sonora said, becoming impatient.

Afterwards, she faced the beloved Queen.

Chapter 18- The Truth

"Isn't it yummy for the soup to have nectar, the finest herbs, fresh mushroom, mountain ashes, squash, and blue butterfly pea flowers?" Queen Sonora answered, ignoring Ely.

"I think it's not extraordinary!... Unless you added something to make it very special?" Queen Isabella asked her again but quite annoyed.

"To make my soup the most precious gift to you, out of real love, I added a few droplets of tears instead of a dash of salt. Fairies hate salt, right? ... This is something unique and memorable on your birthday!" Queen Sonora admitted yet she sounded proud.

"Ah-ha!... Woe to you, I won't vanish! Because I believe they were the tears of the fairy child's genuine love to me and to all who live here. Such for sure saved me. It will create pure joy on my birthday and onwards! Let's not make this long," Queen Isabella remarked.

"That's right! And here is Little Ely who has just recited the poem of truth about you and your evil plan," Auggie said aloud, feeling happy and pleased of his daughter's achievement.

Meanwhile, Dorie hugged and kissed her daughter; her wings ready to protect her daughter.

Ely stopped crying. She held her face and her green wings up, feeling victorious this time.

Chapter 19- The Awarding

Enraged, with the raised scepter of commanding power on her right hand, Queen Isabella drove Queen Sonora away without much thought and consideration. She declared that Verde Hilltop's main gate will be forever closed to the monstrous Queen and her army of bats.

At once, as one community, the dwellers shooed the bats away.

Crazy Queen Sonora and her army of bats flew back to their cold, pitch black cave. All of them were defeated and doomed. They were covered with blanket of darkness.

Meanwhile at the Verde Hilltop, the stars bedecked the night sky, all twinkling and celebrating. They seemed joyful to erase the mysterious and evil shade of darkness. Soon, the party continued. Queen Isabella was so glad and satisfied on her birthday.

To cap the festivities, Ely's family received the magical crystal ball that could foretell the past and the future, and most importantly, that could envision and feel real love and pure joy.

Auggie and Dorie felt so honored and proud of Ely.

There were resounding applause, music, and trumpets blowing. All of them rejoiced for the winning family.

With kindness, love and joy, Ely shared the magical crystal ball to her three, beloved friends- Billy, Miggy and Mindy. She was so thankful to them.

"Thank you, too!" Ely's fairy friends said, smiling with grateful hearts.

"Once more, our friendship was tested, and it was proven as a strong and solid relationship," Ely said.

"We are here for you, Ely," Billy said.

"We are one with mutual support and trust," Mindy and Miggy added.

"I'm so happy that you're my friends. I know so rightly where I am supposed to be... and that's in your company," Ely expressed a piece of her heart.

Chapter 20- Awesome Fairies

"Your tears really matter, eh!" Billy teased Ely again when they were just the two of them at one corner at the party.

"Love matters most, my buddy."

"It has empowered the hero within us, right, Ely?"

"Superb!... And love makes a way to a happier and safer place."

Both of them gaily flew away, up and down, over the hill.

They danced and sang songs. They even sang their favorite song, "Dixie, Pixie and Trixie in my Dream".

They loved to play at night time, but they knew the curfew by heart.

They giggled over the flowers and the grasses which all looked already tired and sleepy.

Together, they wished that humans would see and appreciate them as real fairies and not fallen angels.

Then, out of the blue from nowhere, an innocent looking but anxious boy greeted them, "Hello! I am certain that you are fairies!" And then, he dried his tears.

"Uhummm," Ely and Billy nodded and rolled their eyes in wonder.

"Finally, I have seen real ones," the boy remarked. He had been crying because he got lost at the woods.

The boy did not feel worried and tense anymore. He became at ease, so hopeful when he met Ely and Billy.

The fairy buddies were surprised and unprepared for this incident.

However, again with kindness in their pure hearts, they replied to the boy in a friendly manner, "Hello! Yes, we are real fairies!"

"Uhm, can you help me?" the boy asked.

"Sure!" Billy assured the boy.

"By all means, we can help you. We can also use the magical crystal ball to have the glimpse of the past, to predict the future, to see and feel real love and pure joy!" Ely mentioned her award.

Her hands touched her heart. After all, wasn't she the perfect gift to Verde Hilltop's Queen and all dwellers? All fairies hailed her as the green-winged grand champ.

"But hey, awesome fairies! I'm hungry!... Do you have a bowl of soup?" the boy asked.

"Soup?" the fairies asked and looked at each other.

The boy nodded his head.

Smiling at the boy, the fairies' wings flapped from side to side, and up and down, and their eyes communicated to get ready for their next adventure.

The
End

SPECIAL REQUEST

To all those who bought and read this book-

If you loved this Early Chapter Book and have a minute to spare, the author would really appreciate a short review from you to be posted on the site where you bought or read the book. Your help in spreading kind words is a great succor to other readers, especially to the young children from different parts of the world.

GREAT THANKS!

The Author

Hi! **Lucy E. Lombos** is the author of this Early Chapter Book.

Each letter of her first name has meaning.

L- Light. Yes, that's right, the bubbly light of the family! She is a loving daughter and sister, a wife, a mom of three sweethopes, a jolly friend and a brilliant teacher. She always asks the Holy Spirit to enlighten her mind, to inspire her and guide her all the time. Praise God! Modesty aside, she graduated with Honours-Valedictorian in Elementary, Silver Medallist with General Excellence Award in High School and Cum Laude in College.

In De La Salle University, Taft, Manila, she pursued her graduate studies; and completed the academic units at the University of the Philippines where she specialized in Language and Literacy. She further enhanced her English proficiency skills by enrolling in a TESOL (Teaching English to Speakers of Other Languages) Course with Practicum in Vancouver, British Columbia, Canada.

U- Understanding. She has a substantial and deep understanding of her profession. She undertakes teaching the English fundamental skills, and these are – Speaking, Reading, Writing and Listening. She founded Lombosco Academy in the Philippines in 2000 and she remains the Academy Directress, and the Editor-In-Chief of its Newsletter.

C- Children. They are the subject of her craft. She studied courses about Writing for Children, Writing a Life Story, and Writing

Young Adult Novel in Canada. She also earned a Diploma in Child Psychology in USA. In Spring time of 2020, she enrolled in Child Protection: Children's Rights in Theory and Practice at the Harvard University edX.

Y- Young. She is always young at heart. She would like to learn more. She never stops resting on her laurels. She enjoys blogging and contributing articles for different media. Further, she is a member of ILA- International Literacy Association and Society of Children's Book Writers and Illustrators.

*N.B. *In the Philippines, Lucy taught at Puerto Galera Academy after her College Graduation; later, she became the Principal at Prince of Peace Montessori.*

*Through her authored books, in March 2018, Puerto Galera's Sangguniang Bayan gave her an Official Recognition for promoting tourism in that province; In October 2019, another Special Recognition was awarded to her by the Puerto Galera Tourism Council.

*She always gives and donates FREE Books, and she says, "It's my wish that my books would find their way to all young readers' hands and hearts."

Lucy's Published Books

Ang Tinago Kong Piso/The Peso-Coin I Kept

The Class Lady Bug

The Star of the Sea: A Boat Ride

Happiness 365 and ¼ Days (a biography)

'Ter and Ter', the Turtle and the Eagle

The Joys of Junior

Swanie's Bag

Rose of Calapan (a Novel)

Bono (an Early Chapter Book)

Three Fables, Part 1:

Keys to Change the Heart

Three Fables, Part 2:

Sparks to Brighten one's Purpose in Life Pinky Oinky

Gracie and Dots

After Six o' Clock Nightfall

(Horror Short Story Tetralogy) Noshi

One Drop, Two Drops and Much More Ellie-Phant and

Mon-Keysha

Her Upcoming Books

Monsters in Lazareto (Horror Folktales)

Cotton and Nibbles

Beary G

The String of Saga Seeds

The Seed

BONUS

Dixie, Pixie and Trixie in my Dream

(A Poem, turned into a Song, Composed by Lucy Lombos)

Hope in the newness of morning
Till the velvety dark
Fireflies were brightly viewed blazing
Yet, the night was stark.

The last page of my book reading
Figures formed in mem'ries
Dreams were made up while sleeping
Mopheus, bless reveries!

It looked like sheer joy and surprise
Lo and behold, Dixie.
With wings of faith and peace, arise!
Seemed like upsy-daisy.

There came fayes, Pixie and Trixie
Gleaming in the moonbeam...
The clock's rung, stop, have mercy! ...
T' is nothing but a dream.

New dawn... Go with high self-esteem.
Fairies are mystiques...
The sun is up, face the extreme ...
Get ready for critiques.

Acknowledgment

I would like to express my deep gratitude to the following people for giving me the big support which I humbly needed in writing this book –

Umberto L. Lombos for publishing this book;

Annie Datu-Enriquez for editing the manuscript;

Sining Tañedo-Bruni for writing the Foreword;

Sr. Alice Fulgencio, FMA,

Daughter of Mary Help of Christians (Salesian Sister); a missionary in Papua New Guinea since 2010; Lecturer at St Peter Chanel Catholic College of Secondary Teacher Education, East New Britain, PNG.

Mr. Rizalino de la Cruz, LPT,

Former Principal at Divine Word College of Calapan, Calapan City, Oriental Mindoro from 1996-2006; Currently appointed Principal of Elite International School in Riyadh, Kingdom of Saudi Arabia from 2006 to present;

Ms. Elena Carter, Writer from Varna, Bulgaria;

And Ms. Aissa Custodio-Yeung from Richmond, BC, Canada -

for writing the wonderful blurbs for this book,

And to my family for giving me the moral support.

I am truly happy and grateful to you all.

Without your generous help, this book may not have been possible.

Indeed, the story brings back the readers to the colorful yet straightforward days of their childhood. Full of enchantment and loaded with pure innocence, I love "Ely's Gift". In this tale, I see and feel each character. Everything is richly descriptive. It's well-crafted by Lucy Lombos. Sometimes situations present themselves as complicated. But we can always choose good vs. bad and love vs. hatred. Throughout the book, I was hopeful that good and love would prevail. I hung onto its magical world, willing for good to win. A joy to read!

AISSA CUSTODIO-YEUNG
Richmond, BC, Canada

When Ely, a young fairy, goes on a journey with her friends, where they find out that their queen's life is under threat, she learns how kindness, teamwork and support from friends can perform miracles. Not only does she save her Queen Isabella from the evil Queen of the Bats, she also comes up with the perfect birthday present that Isabella was secretly wishing for, all while making her parents truly proud of their daughter and becoming a full-fledged fairy.

"Ely's Gift" is a book about kindness, friendship, love and joy, teaching the young readers that anything is possible when you put your heart into it.

AUTHOR ELENA CARTER

Varna, Bulgaria